THE TWO O'CLOCK KILLER

ALSO BY NIZ THOMAS

Elder Hunger

Fiona's Mercy

First Light of Every Morning

Lady Death

My Bleeding Kansas

No Control

Paint It Thrice

Rail Music

Ray-Ray's Stoop

Red Tempest

Ships in the Night

Songbird

The Bad Guy

The Climb and The Glory

The Forever-ish Flame War

The Omega Diner: A Ledgerman Story

The Two O'Clock Killer

The Voice of Rage and Ruin

Thin Air: A Ledgerman Story

Upon Your Dreams They Prey: A Lullaby

Vida's Sixth Trip Around the Sun

THE TWO O'CLOCK KILLER

Stimble stretched out in his silver Chrysler sedan. Enjoying the extra legroom of the personal vehicle, having decided against bringing a station-issued one with him to this stakeout. Given he was in a residential area—small but manicured lawns, respectable-looking homes (not exactly your typical stakeout destination)—he hadn't wanted to attract any unwanted attention with something screamed cop.

His gaze had shifted away from the single-level house tucked into the corner lot and toward admiring his vintage Patek Philippe Nautilus watch, rubbing his fingers along the scuffed leather band and the patina at the edges of the round face, absentmindedly thinking about when his Daddy had given it to him all those years ago.

Thinking about the past. And about new chapters. Standard for a stakeout where your mind doesn't have much else to do but wander.

His reverie was broken when his bird—that's what he called his phone—chirped on his hip.

He sat up in the plush driver seat and took the call, keeping one eye on the house. He'd been sitting on it for the last hour, parked just far enough away and in the shadows so if anyone was inside, they couldn't see him move.

"Yeah?"

It was Teddy, his partner. Lead detective on this case. On most cases. Some people called Teddy the Beagle, on account of his eager pursuit of all things investigative. Teddy was the kind of guy that took that as a compliment. Stimble was the Robin to his Batman. It suited him just fine.

"I'm twenty-five minutes out from your location," Teddy said as Stimble glanced at his watch. "Got tied up with this creep Anderson."

Anderson was a shady guy, a lead that Stimble told Teddy wasn't worth running down. But Teddy was by the book. And so he had Stimble come out here to the suburbs and sit on this other lead—this Tim Murdoch, who was supposed to be living inside the single-level home—while Teddy checked out Anderson.

"Wasn't him, huh?" If Teddy was still coming here, Anderson wasn't the guy. But Stimble already knew that.

"Don't say I told you so."

Stimble didn't. He'd jab Teddy with it another time. Instead, he said, "It was the clock was missing, wasn't it?"

"You gonna make me put a notice in the paper: *STIMBLE WAS RIGHT*?"

"Maybe just a spot on the radio. A full thirty-second one, though. Don't get all cheap on me."

"Play your lottery numbers, you lucky bastard."

"Lucky's better than good, sometimes."

"Smartass. Anything moving on your end?"

"Doesn't look like anybody's home. But I got a hunch about this one." Stimble had done some homework on Murdoch. And he liked him for this. Seemed like he could be the guy they were after.

"Sit tight 'til I get there, huh?" Teddy said.

Stimble clicked off. Looked at the house. Nothing doing.

Lights punctured the dark street. Halogens. Blinders, was what Stimble called them. Bright white and blue like they were shining down from heaven, last thing you see before you go into the light. Whatever happened to being able to see on the road?

The car approached from the north, like someone coming home for the night. Pulled into the driveway of the house, opened the garage, parked inside next to a wall of neatly arranged power tools. Stimble's eyes finally came to. A blurry figure in the shadows went to the inside garage door and into the house, the outside garage door closing as he did so. Lights went on in the house, then off. On, off. On, off.

Like an SOS.

Stimble exited his vehicle and walked to the door. Neighborhood was quiet, not even any dogs barking. Not surprising for nine-thirty on a Wednesday night. School night. Kids were already supposed to be in bed.

As he walked toward the front door, intentionally stepping on the grass rather than the neatly placed stone walkway, he noticed the low hum of porch lights and the stronger hum of the occasional spotlight in the yards along the street, lighting up front facades with some blinding, garish yellow light meant to make the house look majestic but really just casting odd shadows around the yard.

Tim Murdoch's house didn't have any lights on outside.

Stimble knocked on the door.

More interior lights turned on. Footsteps moved toward the door. The porch light overhead went on.

"Yeah?" Tim Murdoch said, opened the door. Forty-eight. Single white male. Five-nine, one-sixty. No kids, despite the neighborhood. Shaved head. Nothing special, was how Teddy described him to Stimble after pulling his info. Stimble had said it was always the normal ones who turned out to be monsters.

"Detective Stimble." Flashed the badge, watching for that flicker in everybody's eye. The one where they inventory their whole lives, wondering what they did wrong. And why Stimble was on their doorstep.

He loved that flicker.

"Mind if I come in and ask you a couple questions?"

"About what?"

Stimble stepped in. "I'll be asking the questions, Tim."

Murdoch stepped in and out of the way. Not sure what to do.

"Let's talk in the living room," Stimble said, closing the door behind him.

Tim Murdoch obliged him.

"Can I get you anything?"

"Warm water with lemon."

Murdoch looked put off by the request, which made Stimble happy. Eventually, the suspect padded into the kitchen. Glasses started clinking.

Unlike the movies, Murdoch didn't call out over the clinking sounds. Didn't try to make small talk. Which suited Stimble just fine, since he was already checking out the living room.

There wasn't much to the house. Looked about what he'd expected after watching it for hours. Nice but not sprawling. From the living room he had a good (not great) view at twenty-square-feet of backyard, both bedrooms, the office. Only the kitchen and hallway bathroom weren't visible from Stimble's vantage point.

The vintage bulbs were the first thing that caught his attention, though. How could they not, glowing yellow-orange like a collection of dying flames?

They were positioned on a mantle above the room's lone unlit fireplace. Edison bulbs, though those were easy to come by. Just table stakes for collectors, as Teddy had told him after doing a deep dive online. But Murdoch had others. Amber-hued bulbs the shape and size of an avocado. Smoky Chandeliers with twisted, ornamental filament designs.

Tim Murdoch had quite a collection here.

Stimble checked his watch. Ten minutes until Teddy arrived.

This collection was part of the profile, oddly enough. *Obsession with vintage items highly likely—lightbulbs, radios, cars*, was what they'd gotten back from VICAP. After Teddy had found trace elements of tungsten on one of their first victims, they'd narrowed it down to lightbulbs. Was a weird obsession, Stimble knew. Twenty years on the job, never saw it in any profile before.

Wasn't particularly happy to see it in this one.

The rest of the profile—the age, sex, location details—were already hits for Murdoch, which is why Stimble was here in the first place. He and Teddy had basically been working down the list of antique lightbulb collectors since making the connection with tungsten a week and a half ago.

Since that time, there'd been three more victims.

Stimble had been busy.

He'd also been the one to suggest they split up their efforts, try to catch the killer double-quick. He'd be happy to leave this all behind him now. It was this case that had him thinking about chapters ending back in the car. And what all might come next.

"My guilty pleasure," Murdoch said from behind him.

Stimble turned. Murdoch was close, almost too close. Definitely uncomfortably close, at least. Stimble grabbed the glass of warm water with lemon from Murdoch.

"The filament bulb, Thomas Edison. The appeal of that time period. The *craftsmanship*, even on the bleeding edge of technology at the time. For some reason that just does it for me, you know?"

"Sure."

Stimble put the cup down on a side table. Gestured for Murdoch to sit down on the couch.

"So what was it you needed to speak to me about, detective?"

The guy was cool, collected. Almost too much so.

"I'm part of the task force tracking down leads on the Two O'Clock Killer," Stimble said, using the obscene moniker the papers had come up with. He didn't like doing it, but it was how the general public knew the guy, so it helped with the shorthand.

"Oh."

"And your name is next up on my list."

"My name?"

"Your name."

"I don't see how that's possible."

"Luckily that isn't part of the criteria we consider."

Murdoch sat forward in his seat. "Listen, officer—"

"—Detective."

"Detective. I don't know a thing about the Two O'Clock Killer, save what I've seen on the news."

Stimble nodded, letting his eyes wander around the rest of the living room. The strange thing about the profile was it had identified three components that likely would lead to the killer. *Likely* being the operative word. Unfortunately, a

VICAP workup was as much art as it was science. Just because it said the guy was forty-eight didn't mean he couldn't be forty-six. Five-nine could be five-eleven (though not usually taller than that). It was all more a landing zone than bullseye.

"Would you be surprised to hear that our profile of the killer includes a layman's obsession with applied mathematics?"

Stimble nodded toward the corner of the room. Murdoch had a reading chair setup. Worn-in leather recliner with a side table next to it. One of those arc lamps, bathing the space in a warm, peach-colored glow from the radio-style bulb. Stacked on the floor next to it were mathematics textbooks, as tall from the ground as the armrest of the chair.

Murdoch sat back on the couch, put his arm on the rest. Looked genuinely surprised. "Just because I—"

"You're a numbers guy, I see."

"Not really," Murdoch said. "Mathematics is more than that. A way to think about the world. Logic and reason that underpins the very fabric of our reality."

It was almost as if Murdoch wanted to make Stimble's case for him.

The math stuff was strike two. VICAP said the suspect had a meticulous mind. *Obsession with numbers, logic, mathematics likely.* A mind capable of planning something all the way to the end.

Like a murder. Or ten of them, and counting.

Stimble checked his watch. Five minutes until Teddy arrived. He felt his heart flutter a bit in his chest, his cheeks warm up.

"What is it you're not telling me, Detective?"

Stimble said nothing. Kept his eyes moving around the

room. The words from the profile flitted through his mind like fireflies. *Obsessive. Meticulous.*

Murdoch was a surprisingly strong candidate for the Two O'Clock Killer.

Except for one key element.

"Listen, Detective," Murdoch said as he stood up, "I wish I could be of more help."

"I don't think I asked for your help."

Murdoch put his palms up. Surrender, sort of.

Neither of them said anything for several ticks of the clock.

Three minutes until Teddy arrived. Stimble could practically hear the tires on the pavement outside.

"Wait a second," Murdoch said. "If I'm the Two O'Clock Killer, wouldn't there need to be some clocks here? I mean, I've got one over the kitchen sink. A digital one next to the bed. But check the whole house..." Murdoch's mind seemed to be working, trying to play catch-up. A logician's mind. No doubt there.

He was right, though. The lack of a vintage clock collection was problematic. As stupid as Stimble thought the name was, the Two O'Clock Killer got it for a reason. It was another thing from the VICAP report, though Stimble thought that bit of it was fairly obvious.

Ascribes symbolic meaning to time or timekeeping.

"...I hardly even know how to tell the time on a clock..."

The Two O'Clock Killer left behind some type of time-keeping device at every kill scene. A clock. A sundial.

A watch.

"...so you see, I couldn't possibly be him."

"I think you'll do just fine, Tim."

Murdoch stared back questioningly.

Stimble pulled out his service weapon and shot him in the chest.

Murdoch fell back onto his couch but missed, fell onto the floor. Gasping for breath. His hands were up near his chest, as if trying to plug the leaking air hole.

Stimble checked his watch. One minute until Teddy arrived.

He bent over Murdoch's body as he faded away on the floor.

"You almost checked all the boxes, Tim." Stimble closed his eyes, letting the familiar feeling of a job well done wash over him. Felt the triumph of death tingle on his skin.

Murdoch flailed on the ground and gasped for a breath that just wouldn't come.

"I was worried you might not have an acceptable clock, though." He raised his wrist to show Murdoch the Patek.

Recognition in the near-dead man's eyes. Then terror.

Stimble put a gentle finger to the crown and used his nail to pull it out to the second position.

Took a deep inhale, savoring the moment for a single second longer. Not knowing when he might once again feel this. The investigation had gotten too hot, too much attention. And now he'd have to adjust his process to keep this story going.

The Two O'Clock Killer was now dead. Thereabouts at least. Would be a real red flag if he kept killing people same as he'd been doing.

Stimble wound the dial around until the clock face read two o'clock. Wiped his own prints off the thing, not worrying about the DNA that would be excluded for being at the crime scene. Knelt down and slipped it into Murdoch's pocket as the dying man's eyes went wide with protest.

Death's warm embrace ensconced Stimble, smothering Murdoch for eleven more glorious seconds before Teddy banged on the front door. Stimble called him in.

Murdoch's eyes went wide one last time as he saw another officer of the law enter the room. Stimble knew those eyes were dying to scream the truth.

Dying being the operative word.

Teddy took in the scene, gave Stimble a surprisingly calm raise of the eyebrow.

Inside, Stimble felt like he'd just mainlined the high he usually felt from Death. His partner in the room as his victim died was like nothing else he'd ever experienced before. Nirvana of excitement and anxiety.

What if Murdoch ekes out one last word?

What if Teddy somehow reads the room, feels some of Death's juju lingering in the air like summer static just before it rains?

What if Stimble loses it, hops onto Teddy the Beagle like a feral jungle cat and strangled him while mawing at his carotid in a fit of crazed hunger?

Stimble turned back to Murdoch, the man's eyes recognizing the futility of their plight. It was like what Stimble figured it felt like to watch a baby be born, or one of those once-in-a-lifetime comets shoot across the night sky. He could barely contain his inner trembling, less worried now about his victim unmasking him as he was with crying with complete ecstasy at the beauty of this moment.

Stimble took two quiet breaths. When he spoke, he couldn't tell whether this voice was calm or like a ten year old's who just saw his first naked lady.

"He..." his voice trailed off. He wasn't yet ready to speak.

Teddy put a hand on Stimble's shoulder. Did he feel the

energy surging through? Like a supercharged electric fence for cattle.

Stimble swallowed. "He made a move," he said again, this time confident his words sounded normal. He shrugged, gestured around the room as if to say, *can you believe that VICAP profile?*

Teddy knelt next to Murdoch and checked his pulse. "He's dead."

Stimble let out a deep, relieved sigh that he had no trouble faking.

"But look at this." Teddy showed him the watch.

"Figured we'd find at least one of them in here, once he got squirrelly."

Teddy shook his head. "Wound to two o'clock and everything. The sick bastard."

Stimble shrugged his shoulders, the high of death beginning to drain from him. Usually it lasted for a while, until it once again got too great for him to keep control over.

After this, though ...

He wasn't sure how much longer he could go through life without feeling this again.

"Wonder what it meant," Teddy said, handing the watch to Stimble to take a look at.

Stimble stared into his Daddy's old watch, memories and emotions flitting around on the dying wave of adrenaline inside his body.

"Whatever it meant," Stimble said, "I guess that chapter's closed now."

And another one would soon open.

THE END

EXCLUSIVE SNEAK PEEK

Keep reading for a look at the forthcoming crime suspense novel from Niz Thomas.

FAMILY TREE

A SUSPENSE NOVEL

NIZ THOMAS

FAMILY TREE

A NOVEL

by Niz Thomas

ONE

Joe Parry woke up with a jolt, like he'd just been struck with a cattle prod. His eyes shot open but it took him a second to register where he was. His heart was pounding against his chest like it was trying to escape. Or explode. For a brief second he wasn't sure it had a preference, though his would have been for whichever did the job faster.

He saw a single salmon-pink splotch of paint on the bedroom wall, peeking out from under what was otherwise a complete cover-up job. His daughter, Samantha, must have missed the spot last month when she sponge-painted the entire wall charcoal grey, part of a number of recent changes that Joe wasn't completely comfortable with. He didn't need another look at the nude art posters she'd hung above the eave of her desk for a reminder of that fact.

Joe tried to catch his breath. He'd been dreaming of something dark and ambiguous, a heavy weight of a feeling, like impending doom. Or an anvil on his chest. Unfortunately, he knew the feeling well. He'd had plenty of nights like it in recent years, though this one felt somehow different for him. Worse, sure, but also like the end of something that he hadn't known had started yet.

Turning his neck — which he realized, with some discomfort, hadn't managed to find a pillow in the night — and he felt his heart rate slow a bit, knowing he was at least in his own house. He took a long, deep breath to reacquaint himself with the land of the living and inhaled the orange and lavender scent from the candle he'd bought Samantha two months earlier, and given to her last week for her eighteenth birthday. He felt ashamed now that he'd bought it so far in advance and upon giving it to her, it couldn't have seemed any stranger of a gift.

Even unlit, the smell was so potent it crept through his nostrils and settled deep in his throat, constricting his windpipe just enough to make him cough. Like a feminine version of chloroform.

That scent, and the thought of every moment since he'd first smelled it at the mall, hurt him more than any cattle prod could have. He could see now that two months could move mountains in a teenager's world. Even the two weeks since Samantha had turned eighteen had felt to him more like wrangling cattle than being one. Things started happening much faster and he felt like they needed to be contained.

He could never quite get his hands around the situation though.

Joe put his feet on the floor and slowly pulled himself up. His neck cried out something fierce at the effort and he felt a few muscles down his back and ribcage light up with their own protests, too. He let himself sit there, on his daughter's empty bed, the realization of her not coming home another night made it feel like he just woke up from a car wreck.

Five nights. Five of the longest nights he'd ever had — and that was saying a lot. He wondered if Samantha had ever sat up at night as a kid, waiting in vain for him to come home. He put that thought aside as quickly as he could muster in the cold of the empty room and the darkness of a fall morning. Talk about the shoe being on the other foot.

Sitting there, he picked up the cordless phone next to Samantha's bed. He'd brought it in from his room, just in case she called. It was the only phone in the house and he'd thought about getting rid of it for the last few years but never cared enough to do so. He checked the caller ID but saw there had been no missed calls. He put the phone back on the side table.

He became aware of the tick, tick, tick of his wrist-watch. The rest of the house was silent. A far cry from the city sounds he'd spent most of his life cocooned in. There wasn't a single car horn or emergency siren to be heard. The sticks — as he referred to them, but in reality, what most people would call the suburbs — were far too quiet for him. It gave all the thoughts inside him more amplification than he liked.

He always could have used more of a chance to think before he acted. But sitting in silence, thinking about the worst? Well, that just wouldn't do for him.

Even after two years living in the sticks — a northern New Jersey town called Mendham — he didn't feel adjusted to the quiet. The town wasn't far from where he grew up in Newark, but it might as well have been in another country. The biggest commonality was that people breathed oxygen in both places. Most of Newark was rundown now, but it hadn't been so bad when he grew up there. It was a city of immigrants back then — Italians, mostly. By contrast, the houses in Mendham consisted of a few historic sites built by militia men during the Revolutionary War surrounded by lawyers' and bankers' mansions built sometime after the last bull market. The legacy was still alive, Joe supposed, but the reality was that, despite the fact that just a few miles away George Washington and his army camped during the winter of 1779, the only thing that still remained from that era was the quiet.

And sitting alone in the house his then-wife convinced him would be the salve on half-a-lifetime of putting the badge first, the silence of this place felt personal. Like it was made specifically to torture him. He wondered if any of those militia men had felt that, too.

He got up and smoothed out the bed's comforter, wanting the room to feel exactly how Samantha left it whenever she decided to come back home. Then he went to the threshold of the doorway and turned once more back to the room, wondering if he was being too naïve. If the thought of her coming back to him and this house wasn't more than a pipe dream.

The room looked so different now. Grey and black color had replaced the pinks and pastels from only a few months ago. But that felt like another lifetime at this point. Samantha's closet, neater than any kid's he ever knew, was more of the same color palette. Black and grey jeans and long tees replaced the rainbow colors of dresses and blouses. And a growing collection of nude art posters.

He closed the door and went downstairs.

In the kitchen, he set up the coffee. Samantha had taught him how to use the thing when she bought it for him a year earlier. It was one of those machines with more levers than it seemed to need — like Rube Goldberg's idea of a coffee maker. At the time, Samantha had been going through a "coffee phase" and he was pretty sure the gift had been more for her than for him. Either way, he had to agree with her. It tasted better than the watered-down version his old drip machine produced.

Joe opened the cabinet above the machine and reached past the decaf and lighter roasts for a brand called Unleaded Java. It was that type of morning. After loading the beans into the dispenser, he switched the machine on and it went to work grinding them up. It couldn't finish the cup fast enough for him.

He reached for the stereo remote and hit play, not sure what would come on. It had sat silent for the past five days. Since his wife left them, Samantha had always worked the stereo for him. While her taste in music didn't really match his, he felt it was something that brought them together. Especially before she decided coffee wasn't for her anymore, due to the injustices involved with making the beans, or whatever the issue of the day was.

The song that started up was faint at first, almost mechanical in its introduction. There was no singing or words yet, just a low humming sound mixed with the timbre of a factory — grinding metal and power tools. Definitely not the type of music that Samantha would have played six months earlier, but he guessed those days were long gone. At the moment, he didn't care about the music. He just wanted the noise. The song had an eerie quality mixed with the grinding of the coffee machine. It hearkened back to the days when people like him would have been working the factory floor, not much more to worry about than what the wife was making for dinner that night. But then, he guessed those days were long gone now, too.

Joe stood there, eyes closed, letting the sounds wash over him. For a moment, he fell into a trance, thankful for the brief respite from his own mind.

Once the machine was done, Joe took a big sip of the coffee, the bitter smell and taste bringing back the closed throat feel from the candle in Samantha's room. He hardly noticed, though, desperate to wake up. The song kept playing, growing in intensity, leading him toward something dark and mysterious. He felt like he was moving toward the end of a hallway in a horror movie.

His phone buzzed on his hip, making him jump and almost spill, and pulling him up and out of the trance-like state the music created. He lifted the remote and turned it off.

"Parry."

"Joe, it's Shea," the voice said. Shea Walters. With the music and the fog from a shit night of sleep on his mind, he'd forgotten she said she'd get back to him today. She was a private investigator who used to work undercover with him. A good, reliable cop, though she'd had a bit of a fall from grace in recent months, from his understanding of things. He knew the feeling well enough — his move out to the sticks wasn't *exactly* a self-less move — and he also knew a cop like Shea wouldn't let it get to her. He'd asked her to pull in a favor with a contact she had.

"Hey Shea, you got something for me?"

"Yeah, I'm doing great, Joe. Happy to help a friend in need."

"Sorry. My mind's a little fucked right now. She hasn't come home in five days. I'm just worried."

"Yeah, well, when kids turn legal, sometimes they rebel. My parents would have killed for me to just slip out of the house for a week. They still, to this day, don't believe I was a cop. I didn't have the heart to show them the newspaper clippings after I got canned, just to prove it to them. Try not to take it personal, Joe. It's probably more about her own thing than anything you did."

Joe wished that were true. He took another sip of the coffee, finally feeling it working on his cobwebbed brain, and went over to the sliding glass doors off the kitchen. Growing up, Joe could never have pictured himself living in a place like this. It was too green, too wholesome. He'd worked narcotics and then homicide for a bit in his hometown. The only green he saw was the money they took off the dope dealers when they popped them. The setting out here was more like something out of a Stepford brochure. Not even the dealers wanted to score big and live like this. He doubted they even had the imagination. And these were the same sort of people who started sculpting fake toys made out of cocaine to avoid detection.

He took another swig of the coffee, having a sudden hankering for a shot of Jameson in it. He stared out at his manicured backyard, the showcase piece of which was a twenty-five-foot tall chestnut tree that sprawled at least as wide, canopying the flowers and hedges planted in mulch on the back end of the property. A single rope swing hung from the tree's thickest branch, an addition he'd made on Samantha's fifteenth birthday. He could practically hear her laughter from that afternoon echoing through the quiet of the house.

It was thought to be one of the last surviving chestnut trees in the whole northeast. It was basically the reason they chose the house in the first place.

"You there, Joe?" Shea asked.

"Yeah, sorry. Just trying to stay positive, that she took off with a friend or something."

"I'm sure that's what it is, bud. I wish I had something to

help ease your mind. Unfortunately, my contact came up empty. The phone's been off since Tuesday night."

An icy fear rose up in the pit of his stomach. That was the last night he'd seen Samantha. The night of her birthday. He wasn't all that surprised that she hadn't turned it back on yet — other than being a teenager and have the phone practically be a third appendage.

"I figured as much."

"How's that?"

"The night she left. We had a fight. It got kind of ugly, the mudslinging back and forth. I would have left it at that, but she decided to fling the phone, too. It got busted up, though I thought they made those things out of titanium these days, so I was hoping it didn't break all the way. Or that she'd gotten it fixed if it had. I know she took it with her because it wasn't on the floor when I came back downstairs. She's got pretty good aim, Shea. If I hadn't ducked, that trace would have led you straight between my eyes."

He could hear Shea laugh on the other end. "A girl that takes after my own heart," she said. "Or my dad's, at least. You think he didn't want a son with a golden left arm, you'd be dead wrong."

Joe watched a squirrel bounding through the grass, into the mulch, and up the front of the tree. It worked itself around to the backside and disappeared from his view. He had a sudden urge to tell Shea the rest of what happened that night with Samantha.

"Well, the Amazin's sure could use one right now," he said, ignoring the urge.

"Yeah, every day since '76."

"So what do you think I should do, Shea? I figured she might replace the thing, turn it back on. Your search would have caught that?"

"Yeah. Even if she used a different SIM card or a new phone. My guy is at the company. He checked it all. And what should you do? Shit, it's hard to say. You call around to her friends?"

He had, though Samantha had recently changed more about herself than just her favorite colors and taste for coffee. A few months back, she started hanging out with a different crowd at school. Artists, mostly. At least that's what she'd told Joe they were. He hadn't pressed her because, well, he didn't think she was preparing to run out on him. And because after so many years working the streets of Newark, the kids out here wouldn't have alarmed him unless they started leaving IEDs along the side of the town's lone main road.

He'd need to do a better job digging them up.

"Listen, Joe, I've got another call. One other thing you might try? Her phone is listed under your account. Check who she'd been talking to recently, see if any patterns emerge or any numbers that might clue you in. Gotta run, though. Let me know if you need anything else, alright?"

"Sure. Thanks, Shea. And let me know how I can pay back the favor."

They hung up.

Joe finished his coffee, but by now it was lukewarm and the bitterness tasted like stomach acid fighting its way up into his throat. He'd spent a few days assuming Samantha was just blowing off steam. Then a few days telling himself not to overreact. But now he felt the cold instinct that something was wrong creeping up the base of his spine.

Outside, a gust of wind blew through the backyard, swaying the rope swing as if a ghost were sitting in the seat.

His little girl was missing.

And maybe not of her own volition.

Did you like this story? How about another one for FREE?

Join Niz Thomas' mailing list for a FREE copy of the short story *The Omega Diner*, which placed Honorable Mention in the prestigious Writers of the Future Contest.

Join now to also get:
MEMBER DEALS & DISCOUNTS
FIRST LOOK ACCESS
AUTHOR INTERVIEWS
LIMITED EDITIONS
AND MORE

Join the newsletter here: nizthomas.com/newsletter
Or by sending an email to: newsletter@nizthomas.com

ALSO BY NIZ THOMAS

ABOUT THE AUTHOR

Join the mailing list for a FREE short story
website: nizthomas.com/newsletter
email: niz@nizthomas.com

Niz Thomas grew up a fan of *The Silence of the Lambs*, heist movies, and 007. Not surprisingly, as a kid he wanted to be an FBI agent, a cat burglar, and a spy. He decided to go to college instead and has regretted it every day since.

Niz is an eight-time honoree in the Writers of the Future contest, receiving a Finalist designation for his short story *Vida's Sixth Trip Around the Sun* and a Silver Honorable Mention award for his story *Call Me Betsy*, set in the True Name series. He is also the author of dozens of short stories and several forthcoming novels, including the highly anticipated horror novella *And The Moon Is Full And Bright*, the dark suspense novel *Family Tree*, and the near-future political cat-and-mouse novella, *Election Day*, all out in 2023.

Join his mailing list for limited edition story art, early access to new releases, and a FREE short story about the mysterious contract killer Ledgerman, star of the upcoming multi-book thriller series debuting in late 2023.

Join the mailing list: nizthomas.com/newsletter

COPYRIGHT

The Two O'Clock Killer

COPYRIGHT

Family Tree

Made in the USA
Middletown, DE
03 June 2024